Beast Quest®

KYRON
LORD OF FIRE

BY ADAM BLADE

ORCHARD

With special thanks to Tabitha Jones

For Thomas and Harry Waite

www.beastquest.co.uk

ORCHARD BOOKS

First published in Great Britain in 2021 by The Watts Publishing Group

1 3 5 7 9 10 8 6 4 2

Text © Beast Quest Limited 2021
Cover and inside illustrations by Steve Sims
© Beast Quest Limited 2021

Beast Quest is a registered trademark of Beast Quest Limited
Series created by Beast Quest Limited, London

A CIP catalogue record for this book is available from the British Library.

ISBN 978 1 40836 220 4

Printed in Great Britain

The paper and board used in this book are made from wood from responsible sources

Orchard Books
An imprint of Hachette Children's Group
Part of The Watts Publishing Group Limited
Carmelite House, 50 Victoria Embankment, London EC4Y 0DZ

An Hachette UK Company
www.hachette.co.uk
www.hachettechildrens.co.uk

Welcome to
the world of
Beast Quest!

Tom was once an ordinary village boy, until he travelled to the City, met King Hugo and discovered his destiny. Now he is the Master of the Beasts, sworn to defend Avantia and its people against Evil. Tom draws on the might of the magical Golden Armour, and is protected by powerful tokens granted to him by the Good Beasts of Avantia. Together with his loyal companion Elenna, Tom is always ready to visit new lands and tackle the enemies of the realm.

While there's blood in his veins, Tom will never give up the Quest…

TO
AVANTIA

PORT
CALM

THE LOST
CITY OF VIGA

WOODS
WITHOUT
END

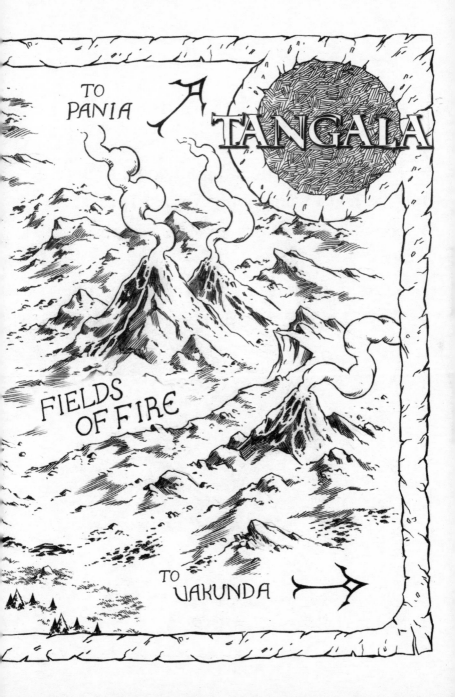

There are special gold coins to collect in this book. You will earn one coin for every chapter you read.

Find out what to do with your coins at the end of the book.

CONTENTS

It is always said that Tangala has no Beasts. That, I'm pleased to say, is not quite true. There are Beasts here – terrifying ones – but they are sleeping. I will awaken them. I will fill them with rage and evil. And I will set them loose on the people of this kingdom.

Vakunda was my prison, but now I'm free. They thought I was dead. They were wrong.

I have lived for five hundred years. I have vanquished any who stood in my path. No puny Avantian boy will stop me now. My Beasts will ravage and destroy Tangala and I will stand over the ruins, ruler of all.

Zargon

THE STRIDING GATE

Tom's legs ached and his head swam from clambering over endless rocks under the baking sun. Having left the city of Viga behind them, he and Elenna were now picking their way through the crumbled ruins of an even older settlement. Tom stopped to push the sweaty hair back from his face, then lifted his eyes to the smoking volcano in the distance, suppressing a growl of frustration.

It doesn't seem any closer at all!

Elenna came to a halt beside him and leant on her knees, breathing heavily. She and Tom had fought three mighty Beasts in as many days, leaving them both close to exhaustion. Each Beast had been unleashed on Tangala by the Evil Wizard, Zargon, using magical weapons he had stolen from the crypt beneath Queen Aroha's palace in Pania.

Tom and Elenna's most recent battle had been against a giant stone cat called Silexa. They had managed to free Silexa from Zargon's curse, saving the cat-folk of Viga in the process. But always one step ahead, Zargon had escaped and was now planning to awaken a fourth and final Beast from beneath the volcano. According to the cat-folk, the volcano had lain dormant for hundreds of years, but even from here, Tom could feel its distant rumble though the ground — deep and ominous, like thunder on a summer's night. *While there's blood in my veins, Zargon will never win!* he vowed.

"How far do you think we still have to go?" Elenna asked, shading her eyes as she gazed towards the volcano.

Tom forced his tired shoulders back and stood straight. "Further than I'd like," he said. "We had better hurry." He took a slug of water from his bottle, but it was gritty and warm, barely touching his thirst.

"There's more smoke than before," Elenna said, frowning at the yellow clouds that wreathed the volcano's summit. "That can't be a good sign."

"It is not," a gruff female voice said from behind them. Tom and Elenna turned to see a tall and powerfully built warrior woman. She was dressed in full armour except for her helmet, which she held under one arm. Her short, spiked hair was pale blonde, and her sun-browned face looked weary, but her sombre eyes were keen and sharp. Tom tensed, ready to defend against any attack,

until he realised he could still see the
heat haze of the desert through her
form. *A ghost!*

Tom had already met two such

spirits, who had each helped him and Elenna reach the next stage of their Quest.

"You must be one of the four brave candidates who perished defeating the ancient Beasts of Tangala," Tom said, dipping his head respectfully.

The woman nodded. "I am Ofelia," she told them. "I fell in battle with Silexa. You have done well to survive the Beast's wrath. But the forces that disturbed her rest are not yet vanquished — Evil stirs beneath the mountain. I fear that before this day is done, there will be fire and devastation."

Dread tightened about Tom's chest like a vice. "Then Zargon must already have reached the volcano," he said. "We are too late!"

The ancient warrior's lips became a thin, grim line. "You are late, yes, but there is still a chance you can stop this Evil. Follow me." She turned on her heel and strode away. Tom and Elenna exchanged a wary glance, then followed as Ofelia led them towards a pile of jumbled grey rocks.

"This was once a magical portal," the ghost said, gesturing at the rubble. "Though it was destroyed long ago, some of its power yet remains."

Tom noticed that many of the rocks had worn, straight edges, while a few were curved. But all were badly weathered and cracked.

Elenna frowned. "As portals go, this one doesn't look too promising. Surely we'd need to go through it?"

"Indeed," Ofelia said. "As it lies, the Striding Gate can take you nowhere. But that doesn't mean it can't be rebuilt." Looking carefully, Tom could see the faint imprint of zigzag lines etched along the length of each brick.

"There's a pattern we can use as a guide," he said. "But without any kind of mortar, it won't be easy."

The woman raised an eyebrow. "Who said anything about 'easy'?" she asked.

Tom and Elenna got to work, sorting the stones into order and setting them flat on the ground, until they had made the shape of a doorway. It looked slightly taller than they were, and wide enough for them to pass through side by side.

Working as fast as they could in the stifling heat, they built the sides upwards, balancing the worn blocks on top of each other. Each new brick made Tom's stacks wobble, threatening to topple them. Sweat made Tom's hands slippery, but soon he and Elenna had two rickety-looking pillars. Three blocks remained: two huge curved sections, and the keystone.

Tom stood back, shaking the ache

from his arms. "Now for the tricky part."

Together they built the arched section on the ground, leaving the keystone until last.

"I'll hold the sides steady while you fit it into place," said Elenna. Tom nodded, then clambered up to slot the final piece in with trembling arms. Even with the strength of the golden breastplate, it was tough work. For a moment, the whole doorway wobbled, but it held.

Ofelia gave a satisfied nod. "Well done," she said.

"How does the Striding Gate work?" Tom asked her, eyeing the precarious structure.

"Clear your mind of all other thoughts, and focus on where you want to be as you step through," she said. "But I must warn you, even

before the portal fell, it was perilous. If you allow your mind to stray, even for an instant, the magic will fail. In the past, it was even known for people to disappear into the gate, never to be seen again. Who knows where they ended up?"

Elenna smiled wryly. "Well, since we're aiming for an erupting volcano in search of an Evil Wizard and a Beast, we probably can't end up anywhere worse. If it's our only hope of stopping Zargon, we have no choice."

Ofelia's weary face cracked into a dry smile that mirrored Elenna's. "I commend your bravery," she said. "And, for the sake of all Tangala, I wish you luck. Now, do not tarry. The Striding Gate will not hold for very long." As she spoke, her form began to fade.

"Thank you, Ofelia," Tom called, just before a hot wind swept across the desert, whistling through the stones of the arch and making it sway. Looking up at the smoking volcano, Tom let its rugged shape fill his mind as he linked hands with Elenna.

Then, with a deep breath, they stepped through the portal...

Tom's foot plunged into empty darkness. His stomach swooped as he fell, his hand torn from his friend's.

"Elenna!" Tom cried, panic rising

as he cast about with his arms, staring blindly into pitch blackness. No sound greeted him. No breath of wind or chink of light. Nothing!

Tom forced himself to focus on his memory of the volcano and breathe calmly, but even the air felt somehow wrong, heavy and dead in his lungs. It made his head spin as if he were drowning. *This is it!* he thought. *I'm lost!* Suddenly, his feet hit solid ground, jerking his spine and pitching him forwards. A blast of heat, fiercer than any oven, slammed into his body and the darkness cleared, revealing a stream of lava flowing past his feet. He windmilled his arms, but thrown off balance,

he couldn't stop himself toppling
forwards — straight towards the
deadly river.

2

AT THE END OF
THE WORLD

A hand grabbed Tom's tunic from
behind and tugged, wrenching him
back just before his foot plunged
into molten rock.

Elenna!

"Thank you!" he gasped as they
both stepped further away from the
flowing lava.

Elenna wrinkled her nose, grimacing. "What is that smell?" A stench like rotten eggs hung heavy in the air, tinged with a sharp acidity that made Tom's eyes water.

"Brimstone," he said, taking in their surroundings. They stood near the base of the huge mountain they had seen from afar. Rivulets of glowing red lava flowed slowly down its craggy slopes and over the ground, spreading towards them like pulsing arteries. The mountaintop was lost in plumes of thick, yellow smoke. Already, Tom's clothes stuck to his skin with sweat, and his head spun from the fumes. He put his arm over his face to breathe through his sleeve. A low rumble echoed from the mountain, sending an answering tremor through the earth. With a hiss, the lava that flowed past Tom bubbled, and a glob of red-hot liquid stone shot out towards Elenna. Tom flung his shield up just in time, feeling a thud as the molten rock hit. Another great bubble of lava rose at his feet and burst, throwing out more spatters. Tom leapt back, dragging Elenna with him.

"That way!" he cried, pointing towards a ridge of stone near the base of the mountain, sheltered by an overhang. Tom lifted his shield over his head as they dodged sideways, feeling more heavy gobbets of molten rock thumping down on the wood. They leapt a crevasse, running a few paces until a sizzling jet of lava erupted in their path, forcing them to double back. Grabbing Elenna's hand, Tom ducked left, diving

between two plumes of shimmering steam, so close he felt their scalding heat through his tunic. Then, with lava spitting and bubbling all around them, they made a final dash for the shelter of the overhang. There they slammed their backs against mountainside and looked back the way they had come. Barren rock crisscrossed with veins of flowing lava reached far into the distance. Cracks and holes pockmarked the terrain, belching out sulphurous yellow smoke and shimmering clouds of gas.

"It's like the end of the world," Elenna said, her voice croaky with the fumes.

"At least we won't have to worry about Zargon harming any innocent people," Tom said. "Surely no one could live in a place like this."

"Pssst!" a voice hissed from behind them. Tom spun to see a small pale face with wide black eyes peering through a crack in the rock. *A child?* "Hurry!" the young voice said. "Come inside. It is not safe out there." The face vanished, then reappeared, glancing around the side of an outcrop. The child beckoned, then vanished again. With a belching, bubbling hiss, another burst of lava erupted nearby.

"Quick!" Tom said. He and Elenna leapt behind the outcrop, finding

another narrow opening in the rock.
Tom squeezed through first, then
Elenna. The child – a boy of around
eight – waited for them in the half-
darkness. Thick, black hair hung to
his chin, framing his narrow face.
His skin was so pale it looked almost
translucent, but his eyes were inky
– completely black, with no whites
nor irises. Swallowing his alarm at
the child's strange appearance, Tom
managed a smile.

"Thank you!" he said. "You just
saved our lives."

The earth shuddered underfoot, and
a deep echoing groan rumbled all
around them, seeming to come from
the rock itself. A few chips of stone

pattered to the ground.

"We cannot stop here," the boy said. He sprinted away, and Tom and Elenna jogged after him. The heat was so intense, Tom was soon sweating fiercely, his breath coming in short gasps. But as they travelled along dim tunnels, deep into the mountain, he felt a breeze stir against his skin. It was warm, but clean. He took a tentative breath though his nose, and caught a faint scent, like summer flowers. *That can't be right!* Before long, he noticed a gentle, gold-green glow up ahead. The light grew steadily brighter as they pounded onwards, until he could make out tendrils of greenery running down the tunnel walls. Pale flowers in creams, pinks and mauves bloomed along the stems and soon the hot air smelled as sweet as on a summer's day.

Suddenly, the tunnel walls opened into a huge, cavernous space. Tom and Elenna stopped at the boy's side and stared in wonder. They were inside an immense cave filled with lush, leafy plants, some as tall as trees. Sunlight slanted through wide cracks in the ceiling far above, and a gentle mist rose from the ground. People dressed in glittering, patterned robes moved between the plants, watering the roots from silver vessels, or picking ripe berries

and other fruits that Tom didn't recognise.

The young boy stopped and turned. "Welcome to our home," he said, smiling shyly as he dipped his head in a bow. Tom noticed that the

loose, patterned robes and cloak he
wore were made entirely from tiny
glittering beads. He gazed around at
the cavern and saw colourful murals
had been painted on the walls. All
depicted a magnificent winged horse,

its coat and wings a gleaming white-gold like the sun, and its mane a blaze of burnished copper and bronze. *Can that be the Beast Zargon means to awaken?* Tom wondered.

He pointed. "What creature do those pictures show?" he asked the boy.

The child frowned, as if puzzled by the question. "Why...Kyron, Lord of Fire, of course," he said. Some of the people tending the huge underground garden had stopped in their work. All had clear pale skin and coal-black eyes, just like the boy. A slender woman, slightly built but with the proud bearing of a leader, strode towards them. A silver crown set with a sparkling stone rested on her long, dark hair. She wore the same beaded robes as the others.

She smiled, and bowed her head, before raising her eyes to Tom and Elenna. "I am Murea," she told

them. "I see you have already met my brother, Zak. I am very pleased to welcome you to our home — although it is very strange. We have not had guests for many centuries, and now we have three visitors in one day!"

"Three?" Tom said sharply, his pulse quickening.

The woman nodded, her brows pinched together. "Yes. You seem alarmed?"

"Can you describe your other visitor?" Elenna asked her.

"Of course," Murea said. "He was of middle age, but not yet grey. He was dressed very strangely: all in black, with a thick heavy cloak – which could not have been comfortable." Tom had to agree. Even wearing just a light tunic, his skin was streaming with sweat. "The man would not stay, although we offered him shelter and food," Murea went on. "We would be glad to offer you the same." The woman smiled, her eyes so wide and hopeful, Tom felt sorry as he shook his head.

"Thank you, but we cannot stay," he told her. "The man you met earlier is an Evil Wizard, and unless we stop him, he will awaken Kyron."

Murea looked startled, but not afraid. "But that is impossible!" she said. "Kyron passed into his final sleep many centuries ago. Only his bones remain, deep within this mountain. We honour his memory by keeping his resting place safe and beautiful. You may as well speak of awakening the mountain itself!"

At that moment, the ground gave a terrific jolt and an ominous groan echoed through the chamber. Murea's smile faltered.

"The mountain seems to be waking," Tom said. "And unless we stop Zargon, everyone here is in terrible danger."

3

RIVER OF ACID

Another, stronger tremor rocked the cavern. Tom heard gasps of alarm and even a few yelps from the folk tending the plants.

Murea frowned, but still looked uncertain. "But…we do not fear Kyron," she said. "He is a kind spirit. He will not harm us."

"Not normally, perhaps," Tom said.

"But Zargon enchants the Beasts he awakens. Kyron will attack, and destroy everything in his path, just like the other Beasts we have faced. You must tell all your people to flee. They will not be safe inside the mountain."

Murea shook her head, her dark eyes filled with alarm. "You have seen the land outside our mountain. There is nothing for us there. And many have never left these caverns. We belong here. We cannot just go!"

"Then you must tell your people to hide until we have dealt with Zargon," Elenna told her. A *boom* caused the chamber to quake, and this time, many people screamed,

ducking for cover beneath the tree-
like plants.

"We need to find Zargon at once
if we are to stop him," Tom told
Murea. "Can you take us to where
Kyron is buried?"

Murea nodded. Then she raised
her voice. "We are in danger!" she
cried. "Everyone head towards the
stores!" The cavern erupted with
movement and worried murmurs.
Murea beckoned Tom and Elenna.
"Come!" she said.

They followed Murea around
the walls of the huge cavern until
they reached an archway on the far
side. Tom could hear the rush and
slap of water against stone from

beyond the entrance. It led into a wide, dim tunnel where a steaming river, spitting with bubbles, flowed into darkness. Shallow, bowl-shaped coracles with long poles waited at the river's edge. Each of the circular boats was covered in glittering chips of red and green stone, so they shone like jewels in the low light. Murea pushed one of the boats into the river and beckoned for Tom and Elenna to climb aboard.

"Be careful not to touch the water," she told them. "My robes protect me from the heat and acid, but the cloth you wear will not." The tiny coracle bobbed and tipped as Tom got in. He could feel the furious rush of the

water through the wood. Hot steam
instantly plastered his hair to his
scalp, and fumes made his eyes sting.
He gave Elenna his hand and they
took their seats as Murea pushed off
from the shore.

The river carried them quickly, tugging them around sharp bends and down steep, water-smoothed slopes, swirling the little boat so fast, Tom soon felt sick and dizzy from the movement and the toxic gasses. Hot water spattered his tunic and stung his skin, and again and again he had to shake his head to focus as the fumes made his vision swim. Elenna blinked hard, her face pale as if she might pass out and her brow beaded with sweat. Murea, staring hard into the darkness, seemed strangely unaffected.

Another groan shook the mountain, making the water slosh from side to side in its channel,

rocking the coracle. Tom gripped the
boat's side, his stomach rolling and
his knuckles white as he braced his
muscles to keep from falling in. The
boat pitched and rolled, spinning

wildly, speeding up as the tunnel narrowed.

"Duck!" Murea cried. Tom lowered his head just in time to avoid a low bulge in the ceiling. The passage widened again, and the boat slowed enough for Tom to make out stalactites jutting from the roof like crystal teeth, lit by a red glow from up ahead.

"Here!" Murea said at last as the river flowed into a wide pool. Using her pole, she pushed them up on to a stone beach, where the boat came to rest with a grating sound. The red light deepened. Tom could see now that it shone through a wide archway ahead of them.

"That is where Kyron lies," Murea said, stepping lightly from the boat. "I will take you to him."

"Wait!" Tom said, staggering after her, catching his balance as his senses swam. "Zargon is dangerous. Let me go first." He hurried to the opening with Elenna at his side and peered through.

Tom gasped. *We're too late!* Zargon stood at the end of a wide platform of rock that jutted into the vast chamber ahead. Crystal pillars – stalagmites the size of grown men – rose from the cavern floor, almost meeting sharp points of rock hanging from the ceiling. At Zargon's feet, in a huge, crescent-shaped pool, lava

boiled and churned, black streaks swirling lazily across its surface. Tom made out a pale skeleton protruding from the lava – long, slender leg bones, a curved hollow of ribs, and the elongated skull of a horse. *The Beast!* As Tom brandished his blade, ready to attack, Zargon drew a long, gleaming sword from his belt and lifted it high.

"Kyron!" the wizard cried, his voice a wild victorious roar. "It is time to wake and serve your new master!"

4

A DEADLY MISTAKE

"No…" murmured Murea. She tried to leap past Tom, still holding the wooden pole, but he grabbed her arm and pulled her back.

"It's too dangerous," he hissed. "Elenna and I will go." Murea shook her head, her brow creased with anguish, but Tom maintained his grip. "Please," he said. "We know this fiend well. I won't see him hurt you or your people."

Catching Elenna's eye, Tom gestured to a mighty stalactite just inside the cavern and drew back his sword. Elenna fitted an arrow to her bow and they both crept inside. They stopped behind the crystal pillar, hidden from Zargon's sight. The sword in the wizard's hand began to glow as he uttered a strange incantation.

Tom watched, waiting for just the right moment. He would only get one chance to surprise the villain. But before he could move, Murea shot past him with a howl of rage, brandishing her pole like a weapon.

No! Zargon turned, teeth clenched and eyes smouldering with hatred as his free hand shot out, firing a bolt of purple energy that hit Murea in the chest, throwing her backwards into a pillar. She hit the ground with a *thud* and lay still. Zargon was upon her in two quick strides, sword lifted to strike the killing blow.

Tom lunged, swinging his own sword, but Zargon sent another fizzing jet of energy towards him. Tom blocked with his shield, the force of the blow throwing him back into Murea. He stumbled and landed awkwardly, trying not to crush her. When he looked again, Zargon had turned his back on them. He plunged his glowing sword, point downwards, into the lava at his feet. With a fizzing hiss like a geyser exploding, the lava boiled, flowing over the bones.

"Rise, Kyron!" Zargon shouted. "Become my slave!" He tipped back his head and began to cackle, the lava before him bubbling and roiling around the tip of his sword. But as he drew the blade clear, a slender form sprinted past Tom. *Elenna!* She reached the cackling wizard and shoved him hard between the shoulder blades, cutting him off mid-laugh, and catapulting him forwards. With a hideous scream, arms wheeling hopelessly, Zargon tumbled into the lava, his clothes kindling as he sank beneath the deadly molten rock. One hand broke the surface, stiff fingers splayed, before vanishing again. Silence filled the cave, broken only by the slap of lava on stone.

Elenna turned, pale with horror, her hands shaking. "I...didn't know what else to do," she said. "I had to stop him waking Kyron." Tom stared in shock at the space where Zargon had been. He nodded slowly. Killing his enemies was always his last intention, but Elenna was right. It was the only option they'd had.

"He can't hurt anyone now," he muttered.

A shimmering movement behind Elenna caught his eye. A ghostly form appeared – a tall, broad-chested man, glowing with a pale blue light. The man was clearly a warrior, dark-skinned, armoured and immensely muscular, with a thick beard and

tightly curled hair. But it was his
expression that captured Tom – a
wide-eyed look of pure terror.

"It's not that simple," the man said,
in a deep, hollow voice. "I am Angis.
I defeated Kyron long ago. But I fear
you have now created something far
more terrible."

"What do you mean?" Tom asked.

Angis turned and gestured towards
the lava, which had begun to glow
so brightly, it made Tom wince. And
now he could see Kyron's bones,
rising from the surface, shining like
the sun. The horse's legs wheeled, as
if he was trying to gallop, and with
a heave of gleaming muscles, he
pushed himself up, lava streaming

from his body. *No…not Kyron's body…*

Tom gasped with horror. For the horse-Beast did not have a horse's head, but a human's torso in its place. And the visage was a familiar one. The face was that of Zargon himself! Somehow he had been fused with the Beast; not dead at all, but another creature entirely. His bare chest and arms blazed with light, and his eyes glowed like red hot coals. One human hand still clutched the sword, its blade aflame. As he turned to Tom, the wizard's lips spread into a wicked grin of evil delight.

"What have we done?" Tom whispered.

5

TRAPPED

The cavern began to shake so hard, Tom staggered and almost fell. The Wizard-Beast spread his mighty wings in a blaze of fiery reds and golds, and brandished his flaming sword. He cast a disdainful glare towards Tom where he huddled with Elenna and Murea, then at Angis.

"You fools!" he rasped, his voice

horrible, a crackling hiss, like embers striking water. "Now I am more powerful than ever! You will perish here, beneath the mountain, while I will rule Tangala! No one can stop me now!"

Grinning widely, Zargon rose up on Kyron's gleaming wings, buffeting Tom with a searing wind as he swooped past. Tom and Elenna turned to race after the Wizard-Beast, but Zargon lifted his stolen

weapon, raking it along the cavern roof as he left. Huge chunks of rock and colossal stalactites crashed down behind him, blocking the exit.

"We're trapped!" Elenna cried. Tom heard a bubbling sound and turned to see the lava pool boiling ferociously, globs of red-hot molten rock shooting upwards, only to fall once more, sending out deadly splatters. Tom lifted his shield, doing his best to cover Elenna and Murea as he scanned the walls looking for any escape.

"Follow me!" Angis called, beckoning them towards a crack in the rock, almost hidden by a huge stalactite. Tom, Elenna and Murea scrambled through after the spirit warrior, into a narrow tunnel, lit only by the faint silvery glow of Angis's spectral form. The terrific rumble of the volcano was so loud now that Tom feared the ceiling could collapse at any moment. The stench of sulphur burned his eyes and throat.

Tom followed behind Elenna and Murea, half staggering, half running along the shuddering tunnel. Angis glided ahead, leading them right and left, downwards, then up again. The tunnel floor bucked. Tom stumbled, smashing his knees against sharp rock, then heaved himself up and raced on. His breath came in painful, rasping gulps and he felt sick from the fumes. His head thudded with every step.

Elenna tripped, slamming down hard on the quaking rock. She tried to rise, but the earth leapt, and she stumbled again. Tom grabbed her under the arms and heaved her to her feet, then yanked her back into a run. She coughed and gasped but struggled on. Even Murea, dressed in her protective robes, was slowing. And the deafening sounds of the volcano seemed louder than ever.

Finally, when Tom felt like he'd collapse if he ran even a few more steps, he saw a shaft of daylight ahead. Angis ducked under a low ledge of rock and out into the open.

Tom followed, sucking in great lungfuls of cooler air as he emerged at the foot of the mountain, not far from where they had first gone in. Elenna stopped at his side, bent double with exhaustion. Murea let out a gasp of dismay. Ahead, the streams of lava criss-crossing the rocky plain had swollen to rivers, snaking together, forming viscous, swirling pools.

"Murea!" a young voice cried. Tom turned to see Zak racing towards them from another tunnel. Other mountain-folk emerged behind him, pale and blinking in the daylight, their faces etched with terror. They huddled close together, glancing back at the shaking mountain, then out at the lava-covered terrain as if too scared to move.

"Kyron is destroying everything," the boy told his sister. "Except...he's not Kyron. He's a monster!"

"We have to go back in and stop him," Tom told Elenna, though the idea of re-entering the erupting volcano filled him with dread.

"You can't stop him," Angis said, his voice heavy with despair. "You will burn, just as I did."

But seeing the desperation in Murea's eyes, and in Zak's, knowing that all their existence – their home, their livelihood, everything – was inside the mountain, Tom couldn't let them down.

"We have to try!" he told Elenna. She nodded, and together, they headed back into the smoky dimness. They followed the path Zak had first shown them, and soon heard the clatter of hoofbeats above the din of the volcano. Tom raised his sword and Elenna readied her bow as they burst into the cavern where the garden had been. Chaos greeted them. Flames engulfed many of the trees, while others had been lopped down. Zargon swung his flaming sword right and left, slashing though precious crops and setting flowering bushes alight.

"Stop!" Tom cried, charging

forwards. Zargon grinned and
wheeled around as Tom approached,
swinging his fiery sword. The blades
met with a force that buckled Tom's

arm, throwing him backwards. Elenna fired an arrow, but the Wizard-Beast reared up out of the way, and the missile sailed past.

"I told you, you snivelling runts are no match for me!" Zargon spat. With a mighty flap of his broad wings, he took to the air and flicked his sword towards Tom. A jet of lava spurted from the weapon, straight for Tom's head. He blocked with his shield, but droplets of molten rock spattered his sleeves and tunic, burning holes in them. Gasping in agony, Tom slapped at the smouldering fabric. Zargon aimed for him again.

"Here!" Elenna called from behind

an enormous stalagmite. Tom leapt to her side, just dodging the flaming arc Zargon had let fly. As they huddled together, Zargon's face twisted with spite, and he fired a jet of lava at the tunnel-mouth behind them, filling it with quickly hardening rock.

"What now?" Elenna asked Tom, glancing fearfully at the blocked exit. But it was Zargon's hideous rasp that answered:

"Now you will burn, just as Angis did before you – and so will your precious queen. All of Tangala will cower before me! And Avantia too!" He struck the cavern wall with the edge of his sword, carving a deep and jagged crack. Lava spewed from

the opening, pouring into the cave.
More cracks appeared, tracing down
the walls, and soon molten rock was
flowing into the cave from every
direction. "Come out and fight!"
Zargon cried. "Come out and perish!"

1

6

A LEAP FOR FREEDOM

Torrents of magma poured into the cavern, smothering bushes heavy with fruit, and setting flowering vines alight. Tom scanned the walls, searching for any escape. But superheated steam billowed from the tunnel at the back where the river flowed, and the magma was spreading fast, covering the ground. Tom looked up to see patches of impossibly calm, blue sky outlined by the rock far above.

"I'll jump," Tom told Elenna. "Climb on to my back."

"But it's too far!" Elenna said. "You'll never make it carrying me. You go. Save those people. I'll find another way out."

Tom shook his head. "We go together, or not at all." Elenna gritted her teeth, but then smiled.

"Let's do it!" she said, and clambered on to his back.

Elenna wasn't heavy, but weak with fumes and heat, Tom staggered, and had to steady himself. Calling on the power of his magical golden boots, he bent his knees and leapt, high into the air. Flames licked upwards after him and blistering heat seared his skin as he shot

towards the cavern roof.

The Wizard-Beast roared with fury as Tom passed him. He aimed his blazing sword, but missed. The daylight above Tom was now almost in reach. Feeling his upward momentum slowing and the weight of Elenna threatening to drag him down, Tom strained every sinew to reach the jagged ledge above. His hands closed on solid rock, Elenna's weight slamming into his back as he vaulted up out of the cavern and into bright sunlight.

Tom staggered to his knees as he landed on the sloping mountainside. Elenna slid from his back then pulled him up. "Run!" she cried.

As they both set off down the quaking mountain, Tom heard a tremendous crash. Chunks of stone pummelled his body. He glanced back to see the Wizard-Beast emerge, shattered rock tumbling all around him and his vast wings spread wide. Zargon let out a rasping, evil snort of satisfaction as he surveyed the people below.

Tom could see Murea with her arms around her brother. The rest of the mountain-folk crowded close nearby. The ghost of Angis had vanished, and Tom sensed any help the warror could offer had passed. Tom raced onwards with Elenna, leaping and stumbling down the slope, until they reached the foot of the mountain. Elenna sank to the ground, gasping for breath. Tom looked up see the Wizard-Beast swoop overhead, then land on the rocky plain, well out of reach, a grin of menace plastered across Zargon's evil face as he lifted his stolen blade and plunged it point-first into the earth by his hooves.

At once, the ground juddered so violently, Tom's teeth clashed together. The snaking channels of molten rock covering the rocky plain boiled and churned, brimming over. More cracks opened, as red as new wounds, bleeding lava across the ground.

The mountain-folk cried out in dismay. Zargon laughed, his shoulders shaking with evil mirth. Tom lifted his weapon, ready to fight. But with the fresh burns on his arms and chest throbbing sharply, the sight of all the spitting, bubbling lava made him pause. He thought of Angis – a brave, strong man, destroyed by Kyron's fire – and swallowed hard.

"Look!" Elenna said. "The mountain-folk aren't afraid of the magma."

Ahead, Tom saw Murea and her people spreading out around the base of the mountain, making a stand between the Beast and their home, their hoods raised to cover their hair.

"They're unarmed. Zargon will kill them!" Tom said. "We have to stop him."

"Yes," Elenna said. "But how are they even doing that?"

Tom frowned. The people were striding across rivers of lava as if it were water.

A sudden realisation struck him, and with it, hope kindled in his chest. "It's their clothes!" Tom said. "They protect them from the heat. Which means we might still have a chance of defeating Zargon!" The youngest of the mountain-folk, Zak, had taken a place near the back of the group. "Zak!" Tom called to him. The boy turned. "I can defeat this Beast," Tom shouted. "But I need to borrow some of your clothes. I need protection against the lava!"

The young boy nodded, and quickly hurried towards them, shrugging off the long, hooded cloak that covered his glittering robes. "Take this," Zak said, his eyes looking huge in his small, pale face. "But please, save our mountain."

Tom nodded. "While there's blood in my veins," he vowed.

7

THE FINAL STAND

Tom shrugged the heavy, supple cloak over his shoulders and fastened it about his throat. The cool weight of it felt instantly reviving, but made it harder to wield his sword. *It can't be helped!* he thought.

Tom glanced up to see that the Wizard-Beast had taken to the air once more and was flying back and forth, crowing with glee at the chaos he had created.

"Now all we need to do is get him to come down to our level," Tom muttered grimly.

"Leave that to me," Elenna said. She notched three arrows to her bow all at once, then dipped the tips into the lava at her feet. "Go!" she told Tom.

Tom nodded, then set off at a run, passing quickly through the line of mountain-folk and out on to the lava-covered plain. He leapt swollen channels of molten rock, and ducked between plumes of gas, until he was far enough from the mountain-folk

to risk angering Zargon.

"Come and fight!" Tom cried,
waving his sword. "Or are you too
afraid to face me now that I have
protection against your stolen
weapon?"

Zargon glared down at Tom, his lips twisted into a cold sneer of contempt. "I fear nothing!" he cried. "I am Wizard and Beast in one – I have power beyond your wildest dreams!" He aimed his blazing sword at Tom and fired a sizzling burst of lava. Tom sidestepped, dodging the strike. At the same moment, Elenna's bow twanged. Her flaming arrows whizzed through the air. Two missed their mark, but the third struck one of Kyron's outspread wings and lodged there. The Beast's wingbeats faltered. Zargon's face crumpled with agonised fury. As he screeched with anger, his injured wing folded, and he began to fall in juddering jolts towards the ground.

When the Wizard-Beast landed
in a clatter of hooves, Tom charged,
drawing back his blade and aiming
a two-handed blow for Kyron's
muscled flank. Zargon twisted
sharply and lifted his own weapon to
parry the blow. As the blades clashed,
burning drops of magma cascaded
over Tom, but they landed on his
borrowed cloak, and fell harmlessly
to the ground. *It works!*

With new confidence, Tom swung
again, aiming high for Zargon's bare,
human chest. The wizard raised
his sword to block, and seeing an
opening, Tom sank into a crouch and
hacked instead for Kyron's foreleg.

This time, his blow hit home, slicing
a bleeding cut.

The Wizard-Beast wheeled back,
snorting with pain. Tom pressed his
advantage, jabbing again for the
horse's leg, but the Beast reared

and kicked out wildly. Tom leapt
aside, barely dodging the hooves.
Teeth gritted with fury, Zargon
sent his sword whistling down. Tom
blocked, then spun away and lunged
again, his blade slicing through
the air. Zargon met his attack,
steel clashing against steel, sparks
arcing away. Tom fell back, panting
hard, looking for any weak spot in
Zargon's defence. But with his extra
height and crushing hooves, the
Wizard-Beast had greater reach and
power.

"Had enough?" Zargon sneered.

"Never!" Tom cried. Then, calling
on the sword skills from his magical
golden gauntlets, Tom drew back

his blade and charged. The Wizard-
Beast smiled almost lazily, his
flaming weapon ready to meet Tom's
attack. But, at the last possible
moment, Tom threw himself down
into a skid, passing right between
the Beast's powerful forelegs and

raking his sword across Kyron's soft underbelly. Hot droplets of blood spattered Tom's face as he emerged at the Beast's rear. He turned to see Zargon howling in pain and anger as his horse-body reared high, giant forehooves kicking at the empty air.

And now Tom saw something that made him smile. Beyond the Beast, standing straight in the shadow of the mountain, Elenna waited with another lava-tipped arrow ready in her bow. Her eyes narrowed as she found her mark and let the arrow fly.

Thunk! The missile sank deep into Zargon's muscular sword-arm, piercing through the sinews and flesh. The wizard roared in agony, dropping his stolen sword. Tom lunged, hacking for the Beast's rear, but the horse bucked, his back hooves slamming into Tom's shoulder, knocking the sword from his grip. He staggered back, gasping with pain.

"Look out!" Elenna screamed. Still unbalanced by the blow, Tom glanced back to see a pool of bubbling lava right behind him. He tried to catch himself, wheeling his arms as he teetered on the edge; but at the same moment, the Beast's massive hooves came crashing down. His tail whipped past Tom as he fell. Seeing his only chance, Tom grabbed it with both hands. The Beast bucked again, yanking Tom from his feet and sending him flying. Tom tried to tuck into a ball but his head cracked hard against the ground as he landed. He shook the stars from his vision, only to see Zargon grinning with triumph as he loomed.

The wizard lifted his good hand, purple energy crackling around his fingers.

Tom stared in horror. *I've failed... If he kills me, all of Tangala will be lost!*

But then something bright flickered on the ground at the edge of his vision. He turned his head to see Zargon's fallen sword lying just in reach. Tom snatched it up, agony searing his palm as he gripped the burning hilt. Ignoring the pain, Tom sprang up in one fast movement, swinging the blade with all his strength towards the join where Zargon's body met Kyron's.

The blade bit deep and true, slicing

a wide arc where human flesh and
horse merged. Zargon's blazing red
eyes widened. "What have you…"

His words dried up as his mouth opened and closed in wordless surprise. Then his body began to blacken, like paper thrown into a fire. His eyes rolled up, turning white for a moment, before his entire form crumpled into a husk of ash. Then that too disintegrated, catching the wind and scattering before it even hit the ground.

The space where Zargon had been shimmered and blurred. Tom blinked and refocussed, to find a shining gold-white stallion gazing back at him. And in the stallion's eyes, Tom could see no hate or menace at all. It was Kyron only.

Zargon was no more.

1

BETTER TOGETHER

Kyron lifted his magnificent head and let out a high, keening whinny.

Evil has laid waste to my home, Kyron cried, speaking into Tom's mind in a voice filled with sorrow. Tom bowed his head and put his hand to the red jewel in his belt.

I am sorry, my friend, he told the Beast. *I did everything I could...*

But looking around at the lava-
blighted rock, and glancing back at
the mountain behind him, covered
in cracks and flowing with magma,
Tom felt cold and hollow to his core.
The mountain-folk had dropped
to their knees, heads bowed to
honour Kyron. *But their home was
devastated. How will they live?*

Kyron whickered softly, and gently
touched his nose to Tom's shoulder.
Do not worry, Master, the winged
Beast said. *I understand. You have
done enough. I can do the rest.*
Kyron opened his broad wings and
leapt into the air. Tom saw at once
that they were restored, with no
mark where Elenna's arrow had

struck. The stallion rose higher and
higher, like a bright, blazing star
of hope above the wreckage below.
He circled the mountain, tossing
his flowing mane and letting out
resounding snorts and neighs.

Elenna stepped to Tom's side and put a hand on his shoulder.

"Everything's changing!" she said, her voice filled with wonder. And Tom saw that she was right. The lava that covered the parched stone was retreating in its channels, flowing away into the mountain. Cracks closed, leaving no trace, and fallen rocks rolled gently back into place. Soon, the whole landscape had transformed, still barren and harsh, but whole.

The mountain-folk lifted their heads and cheered. Kyron flew up to the very top of the volcano, where a crater still remained. He flapped his wings, hanging in the air for a

moment, his eyes shining like two suns; then he dropped lightly down into the volcano. A final puff of white smoke rose from the summit, swiftly vanishing in the wind. Tom let out a sigh of relief. The volcano was dormant once more. And its people were safe.

"Thank you!" Murea said, running to Tom and Elenna's side. Young Zak was close behind her, grinning broadly.

"We couldn't have done it without your help," Tom told the boy, whose grin spread even wider. Tom handed him back his cloak, which Zak held almost reverently, before shrugging it over his shoulders.

"I am sorry about your crops," Tom told Murea.

She smiled. "We are good at growing things," she said. "And we had many hidden stores – not all can have been lost. There is much rebuilding to be done, but thanks to you two, we still have our home."

Days later, their weary muscles still aching, but their spirits restored by food and sleep, Tom and Elenna stood together in the cool torchlight of the Tomb of Heroes, beneath Queen Aroha's palace. The four tombs desecrated by Zargon had been restored. Tom ran his eyes over

each familiar stone face – Celesta,
Roger, Ofelia and Angis. Each
carved figure held a replica of his or
her magical weapon, the originals
now safe in a secret location, under
lock and key.

"I hope they have found peace,"

Elenna said. Tom nodded, his heart filled with respect and sorrow for the sacrifice each hero had made for their kingdom.

Suddenly, Prince Rotu's hearty young voice echoed down the crypt steps, breaking the peace. "Tom, Elenna! Come on! The feast is starting." After casting a final look back at the tombs, Tom climbed the steps with Elenna to find Queen Aroha and her nephew waiting.

"You know a feast wasn't necessary," Elenna told the queen.

"Don't be ridiculous!" Aroha snorted. She was smiling broadly, her gleaming armour shining in the sun, and emeralds glittering in her hair. "Of course it was necessary. And we've invited some very special guests, so hurry up! You don't need to skulk down here in the tombs! They will be well protected from now on. Never again will I allow our heroes' rest to be disturbed."

Elenna frowned. "About that…" she said. "Tom and I will need to return to Avantia soon. But we hate to leave Tangala with no Master or Mistress of the Beasts. Maybe it's time to reconsider your decision never to appoint one?"

Aroha sighed. "I've been thinking about that too," she said. "For quite some time, in fact. This last attack from Zargon has made up my mind.

I've instructed Rotu to hold trials
to find a new champion as soon as
possible."

Rotu nodded enthusiastically.
"You'll be glad to hear we've
already had lots of interest. Boys
and girls from all over the kingdom
have put their names forward. It
will be a tournament to remember,
that's for sure."

Tom and Elenna looked at each
other, eyebrows raised, then both
broke into grins.

"That's fantastic news!" Elenna
said.

They followed the queen and Rotu,
and long before they reached the
banqueting hall, Tom heard the hum

of joyful chatter. He could smell a mix of savoury scents that made his stomach rumble too. Inside, tables had been laid with gleaming white cloths and covered with platters of bread, meat, cheese and fruit.

Tom ran his eyes across the room and gasped in surprise as the sight of so many familiar faces. Gruff, red-haired Azrael from Port Calm, where Tom and Elenna had battled Teknos, shared a table with several of the cat-folk of Viga. Tom saw Aleesa, the leader of the cat-folk, bend her head of fluffy white hair to listen to something Azrael's daughter, Clara, was saying, then laugh out loud. Aleesa's son,

Ezra, was using hand gestures to communicate with Jed, a youth from the forest where Tom and Elenna had defeated Mallix the snake-Beast. To Jed's other side, Lika and Maya, also from the forest, were busy tucking into plates of fruit and cheese. At a neighbouring table, Murea and Zak, along with others from their home, chatted merrily with soldiers from the palace, their beaded robes glittering in the candlelight and their dark eyes shining.

"For too long, the citizens of Tangala have been living apart in groups," Aroha said. "It is time that all my people became one. We have

much to learn from one other, and many rich and wonderful traditions to celebrate. I hope that we can meet future threats together. That way we will be stronger. And safer."

As Tom nodded his agreement,

something else caught his eye – a
small group of people standing on
a balcony above the feasting. Their
forms were insubstantial, almost
too faint to see, but he recognised
them at once. Stern, beautiful
Celesta stood alongside brave, kind-
hearted Roger, who looked taller
than Tom remembered, and more
sure of himself somehow. Ofelia
was there too, smiling wryly with
one hand resting on Angis's arm.
Angis's haunted expression was
gone, replaced by a crooked grin
and twinkling eyes. The four stood
shoulder to shoulder, gazing down at
the feasting people. And, as they saw
Tom watching, each lifted a hand

in greeting. *Or perhaps farewell.* Tom started to wave back, but the four ghostly warriors had already vanished.

Tom turned to Aroha and smiled. "I think it's a great idea to bring your people together," he said. "Heroes come in many forms, and no Beast Quest could succeed without the help of friends. Zargon might be gone, but other threats are sure to take his pace. But if we work together and support one another, we will have the strength to defeat whatever Evil comes our way!"

"Hear, hear!" said Elenna, clapping a hand on his back. "Now let's get something to eat!"

THE END

1

CONGRATULATIONS, YOU HAVE COMPLETED THIS QUEST!

At the end of each chapter you were awarded a special gold coin.
The QUEST in this book was worth an amazing 8 coins.

Look at the Beast Quest totem picture opposite to see how far you've come in your journey to become

MASTER OF THE BEASTS.

The more books you read, the more coins you will collect!

Do you want your own
Beast Quest Totem?

1. Cut out and collect the coin below
2. Go to the Beast Quest website
3. Download and print out your totem
4. Add your coin to the totem

www.beastquest.co.uk

READ THE BOOKS, COLLECT THE COINS!
EARN COINS FOR EVERY CHAPTER YOU READ!

550+ COINS
MASTER OF
THE BEASTS

410 COINS
HERO

350 COINS
WARRIOR

230 COINS
KNIGHT

180 COINS
SQUIRE

44 COINS
PAGE

8 COINS
APPRENTICE

550+
515
480
445
410
395
380
365
350
320
290
260
230
217
206
191
180
146
112
78
44
30
19
8

READ ALL THE BOOKS IN SERIES 26:
THE FOUR MASTERS!

TEKNOS
THE OCEAN CRAWLER

MALLIX
THE SILENT STALKER

SILEXA
THE STONE CAT

KYRON
LORD OF FIRE

Don't miss the first book in this exciting series: TEKNOS, THE OCEAN CRAWLER!

Read on for a sneak peek...

AN UNINVITED GUEST

Tom popped a fourth jam tart into his mouth and sat back in his chair, watching as couples dressed in their finest clothes swirled across the dancefloor. Shafts of afternoon sunlight streamed through the

throne-room windows, making the
silverware on the banqueting tables
shine. Music and laughter filled the
air. Tom let out a satisfied sigh.

From her seat beside him, Elenna
leaned in close, smiling. "Rotu looks
like he's having a great time," she

said. On the dance floor, the prince bent low over his partner's hand, then swept her into a spin.

"He deserves it after everything he's been through," Tom said. "I'm glad nobody's expecting *us* to dance, though."

Elenna laughed. "I still ache all over from our last Quest!"

Tom and Elenna had recently helped Queen Aroha rescue Prince Rotu from the Evil Wizard Zargon, in the magical kingdom of Vakunda. Now they were guests of honour at a banquet held to celebrate Rotu's safe return to Tangala. Thankfully, they had been spared from wearing formal court dress, though their boots and weapons were polished to a high shine.

Elenna lifted her glass of spiced apple juice and clinked it against Tom's. "Here's to happy endings!" she said. Tom started to raise his own glass but noticed an armoured

Tangalan guard striding towards the queen. The tall, muscular warrior was frowning, her riding boots spattered with mud as if she'd just arrived. Tom's heart sank and he let out a groan.

"This doesn't look like good news," he said. "We'd better find out what's going on."

Elenna nodded. As they stood, Daltec, dressed in a silver-trimmed wizard's cloak, also rose from his seat. He too was watching the guard, his brows knitted with worry. Tom, Elenna and Daltec all reached the queen's table together.

"Your Majesty," the guard said, bowing low, "I have just returned from Vakunda. Our troops have searched every corner of the kingdom, and of Zargon's ruined palace. There was no trace of a body."

Aroha lifted troubled eyes to Tom, Elenna and Daltec. "It is as we feared," she said. "Zargon must somehow have escaped."

Coils of dread twisted like snakes in Tom's gut as he thought of how close he and the others had come to death the last time they faced the wizard. Zargon was one of the deadliest enemies Tom had ever met. The Evil Wizard had been imprisoned in Vakunda for five hundred years, and Tom knew he would stop at nothing to wreak

revenge on Tangala.

"So much for our happy ending!"
Elenna said. She turned to Daltec.
"Is there any way you can use your

magic to trace Zargon?"

Daltec shook his head. "If I had something that belonged to him, I might be able to. But unfortunately, we have nothing."

"Well, wherever he is," Tom vowed, "while there's blood in my veins I'll—"

A chorus of yells and the scrape of chairs being pushed back cut off his words. The music faltered, and Tom heard shouts coming from outside. He and Elenna raced to the nearest window. Far below, guards were hurrying about in the courtyard as purple smoke billowed through a pair of wrought iron gates at the far end. Beyond the gates, the doors to an ornate stone building hung open, with more of the purple smoke pouring out from inside.

Behind Tom, Aroha gasped. "The crypt!"

"Stand back!" Tom cried, then, calling on the magical flight of Arcta's eagle feather, he vaulted on to the windowsill. Tom lifted his shield above his head and leapt...

Clouds of acrid purple smoke parted around Tom as he swooped through the air towards the crypt, angling his shield to guide his flight. He swooped low, narrowly missing the spikes that topped the iron gates, and landed in a run.

Fumes stung his eyes and caught

in his throat as he sped into the half-darkness of the mausoleum and down a flight of steep stone steps. At the bottom, he found himself in a long, dark corridor. Most of the smoke had cleared, but eerie purple light flickered from a side chamber, casting ghastly shadows across the walls.

Tom took a deep breath, then lifted his sword and leapt into the chamber. Zargon stood at the back of the room. Purple light crackled from his gloved fingers to run like forked lightning over the smashed remains of four broken tombs. A pile of weapons lay at the wizard's feet – a sword, a mace, a spear and an axe.

"Stop this sacrilege!" Tom cried.

Zargon's eyes narrowed. "It's too late for that, boy!" The wizard's thin lips spread in an evil grin and he jabbed a finger at Tom, sending out more jets of purple energy. Huge chunks of stone rose from the remains of the tombs and shot towards Tom.

Read
TEKNOS, THE OCEAN CRAWLER
to find out what happens next!

Find out more about
the NEW mobile game at
www.beast-quest.com

Meet three new heroes with the power to tame the Beasts!